Twitta and the Ferocious Fever

ROMANS BY ANN JUNGMAN & MIKE PHILLIPS

Bacillus and the Beastly Bath
Clottus and the Ghostly Gladiator
Tertius and the Horrible Hunt
Twitta and the Ferocious Fever

First paperback edition 2002
First published 2002 in hardback by
A & C Black (Publishers) Ltd
37 Soho Square, London W1D 3QZ

ISBN 0-7136-5962-9

A CIP catalogue record for this book is available
from the British Library.

Printed and bound by G. Z. Printek, Bilbao, Spain.

ANN JUNGMAN

Illustrated by
Mike Phillips

A & C BLACK • LONDON

CHAPTER 1

Going to Market

'Do you like being our cook?' Twitta asked Perpendicula.'

'Oh yes, Mistress Twitta. I mean, it's indoors away from the elements, and I know everyone likes my food. And I always enjoy trying out new dishes,' replied Perpendicula.

'Will you teach me to cook, please, Perpendicula?' asked Twitta.

'You don't need to learn to cook, Mistress Twitta. When you grow up and marry and have a place of your own, you'll have a cook to do it all for you.'

'I know that, Perpendicula, but it looks fun — and I'd enjoy it.'

'Oh all right, if that's what you want. You'll have to get your mother's permission, though. I wouldn't go behind her back. Now, you read out for me what she wrote on that list, Miss Twitta.'

‘Mother wants loads of olive oil, fish sauce, every kind of spice we can get, wine, some cloth, and anything we see that we can’t produce ourselves on the farm,’ said Twitta. ‘Oh look over there, Perpendicula! I can see Verulamium already!’

Soon they were in the bustle of the town, where everyone was making for the market place. Some were carrying huge baskets full of chickens and hares, geese and pigeons. Some had sacks of vegetables and fruit. Others were driving cattle and sheep and pigs into pens. All along the route there were stalls selling food.

'Buy lovely fresh cooked snails!' cried one stallholder.

'Nice plump dormice, all hot and ready to eat!' shouted another.

'Larks' tongues dipped in honey!' yelled a third.

'Can I buy us something?' asked Twitta. 'Mother gave me some money.'

'Oh no, don't waste your money on that stuff. We'll buy ourselves some nice honey cakes later.'

In the market Perpendicula bought huge amphorae of wine, oil and fish sauce.

'All right, Bacillus,' she said to their slave. 'Make yourself useful. Carry that lot back to the cart.'

'Could I interest you in some lovely fresh oysters, madam?' asked a stallholder Twitta hadn't seen before. 'Oysters and mussels, freshest you'll get, brought them up from the coast yesterday myself.'

Perpendicula sniffed them. 'You may have brought them up yesterday,' she said, 'but I reckon they've been lying around for days before that. They'd kill you, those would. Come on, Twitta.'

'I love oysters,' grumbled Twitta. 'That's as maybe, my love, but they have to be fresh or they make you ill.'

But Twitta was soon distracted. 'Look, Perpendicula, olives! Oh, let's get some! You know how Clottus loves them.'

'They're too expensive,' said Perpendicula, moving on.

'That's because they have to come a long way. I'll buy some with my money.'

'Come along, Twitta. We haven't got all day. Time to get some spices. What did your mother want?'

Twitta looked at the tablet. 'Cinnamon, cardomom, ginger, cumin, pepper and saffron.'

'We'll go to my favourite spice shop. It's just over there, in that little street.'

'It looks awfully dark and nasty, Perpendicula.'

'It's the kind of street most people live in, Twitta, so don't talk daft.'

CHAPTER 2

Meetings

'Perpendicula!' a great booming voice shouted out.

Perpendicula blushed. 'Oh, Bibulus, I'd quite forgotten that your tavern was just by my favourite spice shop.'

'I bet,' muttered Twitta.

‘I expect a fine, handsome woman like you got married off since we last met,’ said Bibulus.

‘I’m sure you say that to all the girls,’ giggled Perpendicula. ‘No, I’m not married and I don’t want to be.’

‘In that case, I think you should have a drink with an old friend, on the house.’

'I don't mind if I do – I'm quite exhausted from all this shopping,' replied Perpendicula.

'Twitta, you go and have a look round the forum and be back here when the sun goes behind that pillar. Take care, now.'

'Oh, all right,' grumbled Twitta, and she imitated Perpendicula – 'Oh, I don't mind if I do.' She wandered off, muttering to herself, 'Grown-ups can be so silly.'

Just then a girl came up. 'D'you feel like playing with my hoop?' she asked in a friendly way.

'Sure,' said Twitta, and the two of them ran down the street bowling the hoop.

Twitta was concentrating so hard she didn't notice when she ran into some boys crouching by the side of the muddy track.

'Watch out! Can't you see we're playing marbles here? If I lose this game because of you, you're dead!'

'Mind what you say, she's a Roman,' said one of the others.

'I don't care if she's the Emperor Augustus,' continued the boy. 'If she messes with me, she's dead.'

Forgetting her new friend and the hoop, Twitta took to her heels in fright and raced down endless alleys.

She climbed through a hole in a fence and crouched down to hide. She found she was sharing a back yard with a pig and a goat who were munching on the sparse grass. A few minutes later she heard the sound of feet and shouting. 'Have you seen a Roman girl? Blonde thing with a big nose?... No? Well, if you do, let me know. She wrecked my game of marbles and I want her head on a plate.'

CHAPTER 3

In Hiding

Twitta pressed up against the fence, hardly daring to breathe. She heard the boy stop to catch his breath. 'Just wait till I get you, you stuck-up Roman creep,' he growled and then set off again.

Terrified, Twitta sat in the garden and stroked the goat.

It started to rain.

Soon Twitta was soaked through. She huddled miserably against the fence, trying not to cry. A woman came out with scraps for the animals. 'Who are you?' she asked, looking accusingly at Twitta.

'I'm Twitta, daughter of Marcellus Flavius and Deleria,' said Twitta proudly, despite her sorry state and her tears.

'Oh, Roman, are you?' said the woman, not unkindly. 'So what are you doing sitting in the garden of this poor Briton?'

'I was being chased by a big boy,' sniffed Twitta, 'because I broke up his game of marbles.'

'Big fellow, was he? Red hair and a face full of freckles?' asked the woman.

Twitta nodded.

'Oh, that's Cactus. He's a prickly one, but he's all mouth and no toga, that fellow. You don't need to worry about him. So where's your mother?'

‘I was shopping with our cook, Perpendicula, but she went to have a drink with Bibulus,’ wept Twitta.

‘Don’t they all,’ laughed the woman. ‘Come on, dear. Get up, and I’ll take you back to the forum. I’ll give that cook of yours a piece of my mind when I hand you over.’

They walked through the streets and back to the forum, where the market people were packing up. 'Is that her?' asked the woman, pointing at a frantic figure in the distance.

Perpendicula was rushing around in floods of tears.

'Has anyone seen a little girl on her own? Twitta, Mistress Twitta, where are you? Please come back! My mistress will kill me for sure! Twitta, my darling Twitta, come to your Perpendicula!'

'Here I am,' cried Twitta and ran into the cook's arms.

'Oh, my poor baby, are you all right? Did your bad old cook go off and abandon you? Tell me you're all right.'

'She's all right, but no thanks to you,' said Twitta's rescuer. 'You should know better than to go off boozing and flirting. You're dead lucky I was there to look after her or you could have been in dead trouble – and I mean dead.'

CHAPTER 4

Home Again

At that moment Bacillus turned up in the forum with Clottus. 'Where have you two been?' Clottus asked his sister. 'We've been hanging around for hours. School finished ages ago.'

'The shopping just took longer than usual,' Twitta told them. 'I was very fussy about what we bought and it took for ever. Come on, let's go.'

'Look after yourself, love,' said the friendly Briton, taking her leave.

'I will,' said Twitta, 'and thank you. Here, have this jar of olives for your trouble.'

'Olives!' yelled Clottus. 'Olives, my favourite things! Don't you dare give them away, Twitta.'

Perpendicula grabbed him. 'Now, Master Clottus, you just behave yourself. This lady has been very good to your sister, very good indeed.'

'Good enough to take away all my olives?' demanded Clottus.

'Yes, that good,' shouted Twitta.

As they walked through the forum Clottus looked hard at Twitta. 'You're very wet, Twitta. Something has been going on.'

'No, nothing has been going on,' insisted Perpendicula as they approached the cart. 'It's been raining, in case you hadn't noticed. You take Clottus up there with you, Bacillus. I don't want that boy anywhere near all my precious groceries. Here's a nice honey cake, Master Clottus, to keep you going.'

'Right, off we go!' cried Bacillus.

As they approached the house, Clottus stood up in his seat at the front and began to shout.

'Mother, Mother, we're back! Twitta gave all the olives to a funny old- ' But he stopped mid-sentence because he toppled backwards into a tub of oily fish.

'Clottus, you look and smell disgusting. Bacillus, go and prepare a bath for Master Clottus,' said Deleria. 'And Perpendicula, you had better clean up Twitta, she looks as though she's been dragged through a hedge backwards.'

'I have,' muttered Twitta under her breath.

CHAPTER 5

The Ferocious Fever

The next day Twitta had a sore throat.

The day after, she began to cough.

The day after that, she had a streaming cold and a fever. Deleria decided that Twitta should go to bed and the best Roman doctor should be called.

The doctor came. He put leeches on Twitta to try and cool her down.

'If that doesn't work, give her a mixture of garlic and mustard and fenugreek in the morning,' he told Deleria, 'and sage, fennel and rosemary at sunset. Don't worry, she'll be fine.'

But Twitta's condition got worse and worse as she lay on her bed, tossing and feverish. More Roman doctors were called, but nothing they did made any difference.

Deleria was in tears.

Marcellus stopped going out onto the estate so he could stay near his daughter.

Clottus was too upset to go to school and Perpendicula sat in the kitchen and bit her nails.

Deleria ordered all the slaves and the family into the hallway. 'All of you are to go to your own shrines and pray for my poor, darling daughter, Twitta. She's not getting any better. I don't care who your gods are – whether they're Roman or British or Greek or whatever – but make sacrifices and pray as hard as you can.'

Everyone went off to pray at their own shrines.

Clottus put his favourite toy dog on the altar, and added, ‘I’ll even give you my real live dog, Rovus, that I love more than anyone, except Twitta, if you let my sister get better.’

Perpendicula prayed to the goddess Cybele, 'Oh, Goddess of Life, please, please, help poor little Twitta get better. It's all my fault she's ill. Please don't punish a little girl. Here, take all my jewels and I promise to be a good and sensible person always if you save my lovely Mistress Twitta.'

But Twitta didn't get any better. She seemed to be fading away. The whole household was sunk in misery.

'Is Twitta going to die, Mother?' wept Clottus.

'We hope not,' said his father gravely. 'Now we must take it in turns to sit by Twitta's bed and hold her hand and sponge her forehead. Deleria, you and Clottus go and sleep – you're no use to anyone if you're exhausted. I'll take the first watch with Perpendicula. Off you go.'

'We'll offer up some sacrifices on our way,' sniffed Deleria.

The next day, when Deleria and Clottus took over the watch, there was no improvement.

'I think you should prepare for the worst,' the doctor told them. 'We have done everything we can.'

CHAPTER 6

An Unexpected Visitor

Just then there was a commotion in the courtyard.

'What's going on down there?' called Deleria sharply.

'It's a local woman, mistress. She says she can cure Mistress Twitta,' called up one of the slaves.

'Murder us all in our beds, more like,' snapped Deleria. 'Go away, old woman, we've got enough troubles without you adding to them.'

'Lady, lady, I won't add to them. I heard you have a sick child in the house. Sick – nearly dead, some say – with a fever. I can help you! I have herbs and medicines here, strong medicines made from local plants and good for local ills.'

Perpendicula rushed up to Deleria. 'It's the wise woman of the tribe, mistress. She has great powers. Please let her try.'

'Certainly not! It's just a lot of silly old mumbo jumbo. If our best Roman doctors can't do anything, what can a dirty old Briton do?'

Marcellus heard what was going on. 'Let her come up, Deleria,' he said. 'What do we have to lose? Even I have heard that this old witch carries powerful cures.'

'But it's our little Twitta's life we are talking about,' wept Deleria.

'Quite,' agreed her husband, 'and this woman might be her last chance. These Britons know very well how to deal with colds and agues and fevers – with their filthy climate, they have to!'

'That's right, sir,' cackled the old lady as she reached the top of the steps. 'Now show me to the child. I'll use the ancient cures and the time-honoured wisdom of my people so that your child may live – just you see.'

When she got to the bedside the old woman felt Twitta's head and her pulse.

Then the old woman reached into her bag, took out handfuls of herbs, branches and berries and thrust them at Perpendicula.

'You're the cook here, aren't you?' she asked. Perpendicula nodded. 'Then go and boil these up together in a bit of cider.'

'I could use some wine,' suggested Perpendicula.

'No, we prefer cider,' insisted the old woman. 'Now go and get on with it.'

Soon a terrible smell spread throughout the house. Everyone sniffed and made faces.

'Ooh, that smells just right!' cried the old woman. 'It will work the magic of our great God of the Skies and the Forests. Bring it up, Perpendicula.'

Perpendicula came running with a jug full of the mixture.

'She's going to poison my baby!' shrieked Deleria.

‘No, no, lady, I’m going to make her better,’ said the old woman, and poured her steaming medicine into a bowl. Mumbling quietly to herself, she lifted Twitta up and began to spoon the mixture into her mouth.

‘There, my little one. You just drink that and you’ll be yourself in no time. You drink up old Clula’s mixture. You take in all the goodness of our native woods and our meadows.’

When Twitta had finished the whole bowl, she seemed to be breathing more easily.

An hour later, she coughed.

And three hours later still, she opened her eyes.

'Hey, Clottus,' she said quietly. 'What are you looking so miserable about?'

'Twitta!' he shrieked. 'You spoke! Oh, thank goodness!'

'What are you on about?' grumbled Twitta, 'I always speak.' She looked around her. 'And what is everyone doing in my room?'

'My baby, my baby, you're all right!' wept Deleria. 'We've been so worried.'

'Mistress Twitta!' sobbed Perpendicula.

'My girl!' shouted Marcellus. 'Recovered at last and all thanks to an ancient Briton. What can I give you, my good woman?'

He turned round to her but the old woman had gone.

'I didn't have time to give her a reward,' sighed Marcellus, 'or even to thank her.'

'She doesn't need your thanks,' Perpendicula told him. 'Seeing the child well again was all she wanted. People with healing gifts like that don't want to keep them to themselves.'

'And to think I was so rude and ungrateful,' sobbed Deleria. 'From now on I shall try to be nicer to the local people. You children must follow my example.'

'Yes, Mother,' said Twitta and Clottus.

'Unless they're like Cactus,' said Twitta under her breath.

'Who's Cactus?' asked Clottus.

'Someone who wanted me dead,' said Twitta. 'And he almost got his wish, didn't he?'